How The GRINCH STOLE CHRISTMAS

How The GRINCH STOLE CHRISTMAS

BY Dr. Seuss

RANDOM HOUSE · NEW YORK

This title was originally catalogued by the Library of Congress as follows: Geisel, Theodor
Seuss, 1904–   . How the Grinch Stole Christmas, by Dr. Seuss [pseud.] New York,
Random House [1957] unpaged. illus. 29 cm. I. Title.   PZ8.3.G326Ho   57-7526
ISBN 0-394-80079-6; 0-394-90079-0 (lib. bdg.)

Manufactured in the United States of America   4 5 6 7 8 9 0

For Teddy Owens

Every *Who*
Down in *Who*-ville
Liked Christmas a lot . . .

But the Grinch,
Who lived just north of *Who*-ville,
Did NOT!

The Grinch *hated* Christmas! The whole Christmas season!
Now, please don't ask why. No one quite knows the reason.
It *could* be his head wasn't screwed on just right.
It *could* be, perhaps, that his shoes were too tight.
But I think that the most likely reason of all
May have been that his heart was two sizes too small.

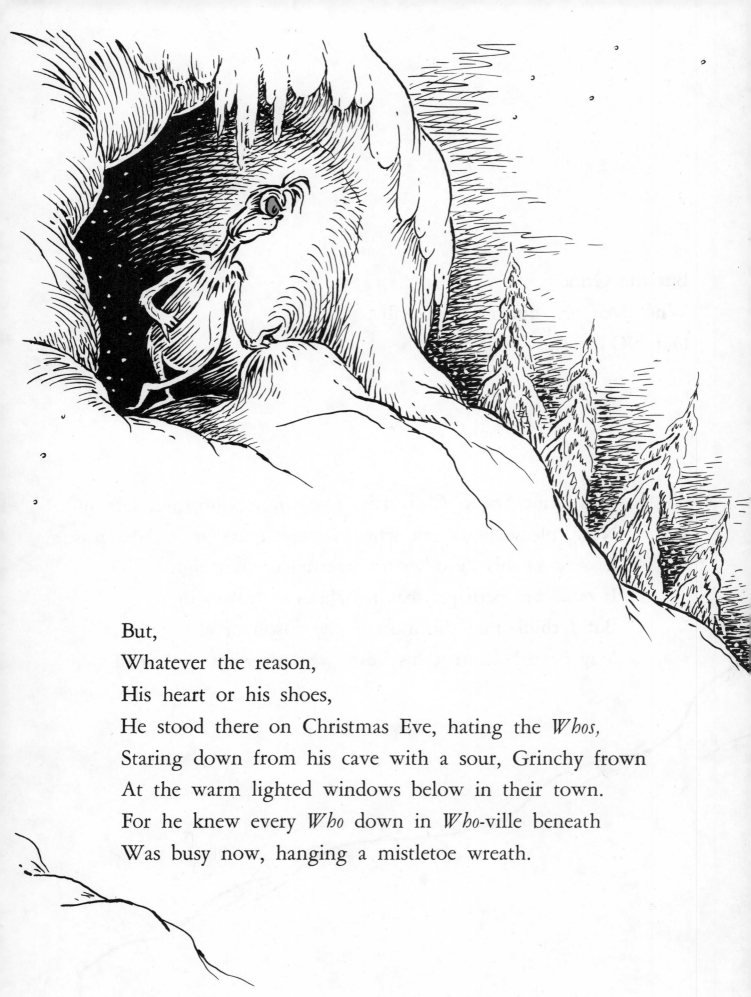

But,
Whatever the reason,
His heart or his shoes,
He stood there on Christmas Eve, hating the *Whos,*
Staring down from his cave with a sour, Grinchy frown
At the warm lighted windows below in their town.
For he knew every *Who* down in *Who*-ville beneath
Was busy now, hanging a mistletoe wreath.

"And they're hanging their stockings!" he snarled with a sneer.
"Tomorrow is Christmas! It's practically here!"
Then he growled, with his Grinch fingers nervously drumming,
"I MUST find some way to stop Christmas from coming!"

For,
Tomorrow, he knew . . .

MERRY MERRY

...All the *Who* girls and boys
Would wake bright and early. They'd rush for their toys!
And *then!* Oh, the noise! Oh, the Noise! Noise! Noise! Noise!
That's *one* thing he hated! The NOISE! NOISE! NOISE! NOISE!

Then the *Whos,* young and old, would sit down to a feast.
And they'd feast! *And they'd feast!*
And they'd FEAST!

FEAST!

FEAST!

FEAST!

They would feast on *Who*-pudding, and rare *Who*-roast-beast
Which was something the Grinch couldn't stand in the least!

And THEN
They'd do something
He liked least of all!
Every *Who* down in *Who*-ville, the tall and the small,
Would stand close together, with Christmas bells ringing.
They'd stand hand-in-hand. And the *Whos* would start singing!

They'd sing! *And they'd sing!*

AND they'd SING! SING! SING! SING!

And the more the Grinch thought of this *Who*-Christmas-Sing,

The more the Grinch thought, "I must stop this whole thing!

"Why, for fifty-three years I've put up with it now!

"I MUST stop this Christmas from coming!

...But HOW?"

Then he got an idea!
An awful idea!
THE GRINCH
GOT A WONDERFUL, AWFUL IDEA!

"I know *just* what to do!" The Grinch laughed in his throat.
And he made a quick Santy Claus hat and a coat.
And he chuckled, and clucked, "What a great Grinchy trick!
"With this coat and this hat, I look just like Saint Nick!"

"All I need is a reindeer..."

The Grinch looked around.

But, since reindeer are scarce, there was none to be found.

Did that stop the old Grinch...?

No! The Grinch simply said,

"If I can't *find* a reindeer, I'll *make* one instead!"

So he called his dog, Max. Then he took some red thread

And he tied a big horn on the top of his head.

THEN

He loaded some bags
And some old empty sacks
On a ramshackle sleigh
And he hitched up old Max.

Then the Grinch said, "Giddap!"
And the sleigh started down
Toward the homes where the *Whos*
Lay a-snooze in their town.

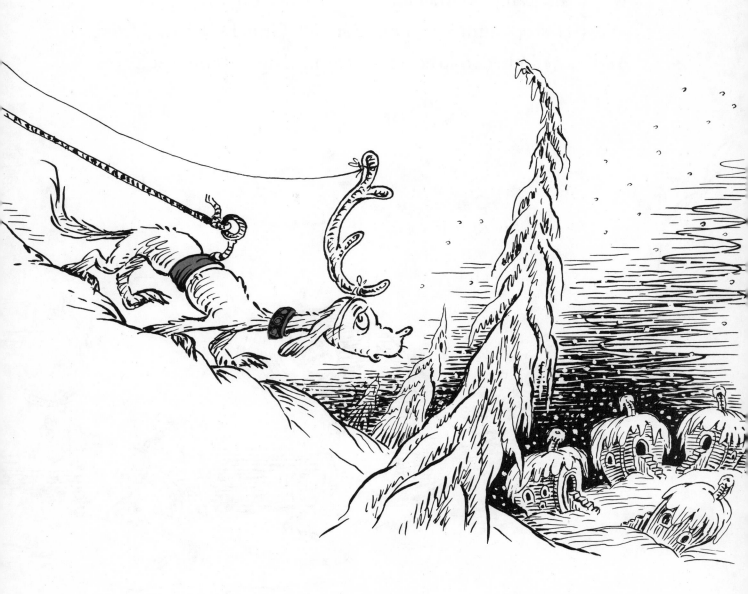

All their windows were dark. Quiet snow filled the air.
All the *Whos* were all dreaming sweet dreams without care
When he came to the first little house on the square.
"This is stop number one," the old Grinchy Claus hissed
And he climbed to the roof, empty bags in his fist.

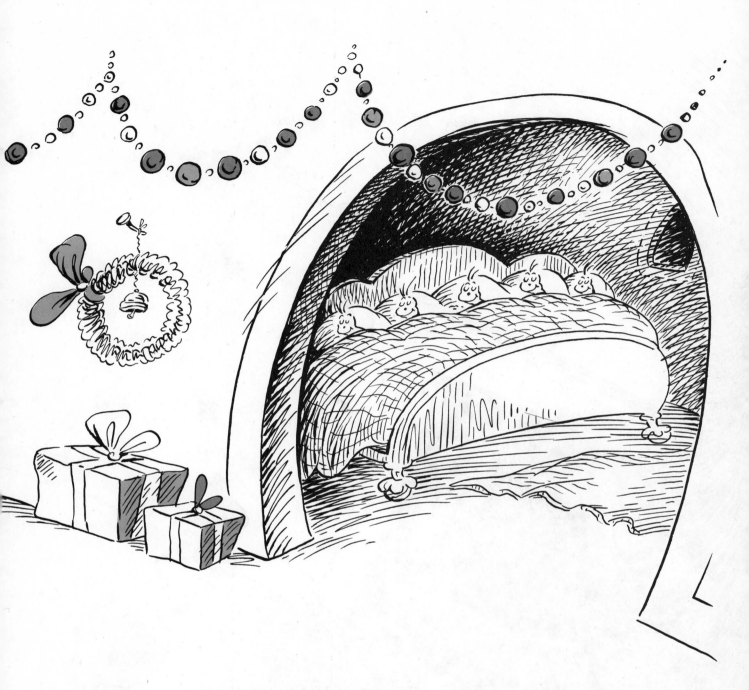

Then he slid down the chimney. A rather tight pinch.
But, if Santa could do it, then so could the Grinch.
He got stuck only once, for a moment or two.
Then he stuck his head out of the fireplace flue
Where the little *Who* stockings all hung in a row.
"These stockings," he grinned, "are the *first* things to go!"

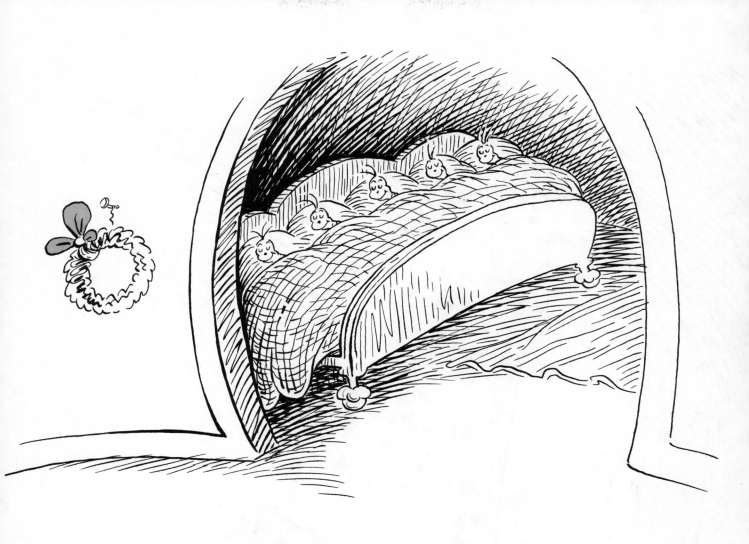

Then he slithered and slunk, with a smile most unpleasant,
Around the whole room, and he took every present!
Pop guns! And bicycles! Roller skates! Drums!
Checkerboards! Tricycles! Popcorn! And plums!
And he stuffed them in bags. Then the Grinch, very nimbly,
Stuffed all the bags, one by one, up the chimbley!

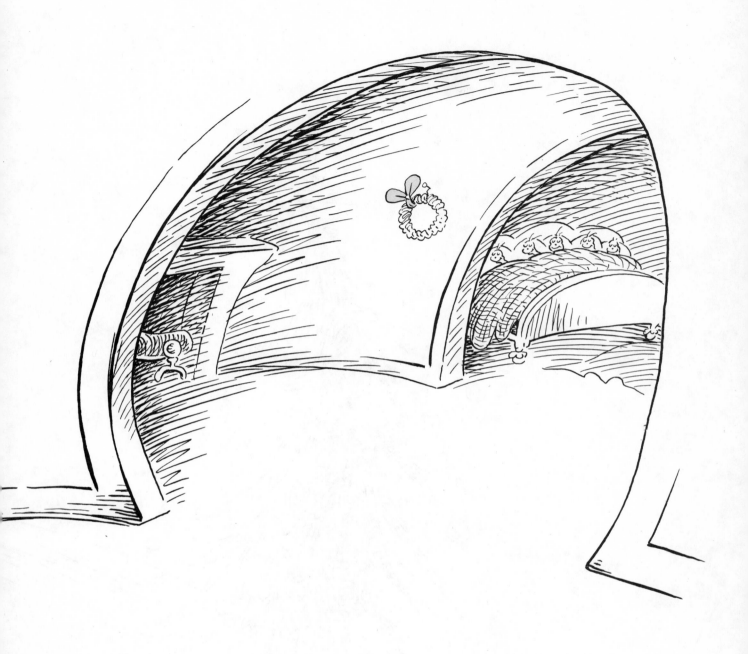

Then he slunk to the icebox. He took the *Whos'* feast!
He took the *Who*-pudding! He took the roast beast!
He cleaned out that icebox as quick as a flash.
Why, that Grinch even took their last can of *Who*-hash!

Then he stuffed all the food up the chimney with glee.
"And NOW!" grinned the Grinch, "I will stuff up the tree!"

And the Grinch grabbed the tree, and he started to shove
When he heard a small sound like the coo of a dove.
He turned around fast, and he saw a small *Who!*
Little Cindy-Lou *Who,* who was not more than two.

The Grinch had been caught by this tiny *Who* daughter
Who'd got out of bed for a cup of cold water.
She stared at the Grinch and said, "Santy Claus, why,
"*Why* are you taking our Christmas tree? WHY?"

But, you know, that old Grinch was so smart and so slick
He thought up a lie, and he thought it up quick!
"Why, my sweet little tot," the fake Santy Claus lied,
"There's a light on this tree that won't light on one side.
"So I'm taking it home to my workshop, my dear.
"I'll fix it up *there*. Then I'll bring it back *here*."

And his fib fooled the child. Then he patted her head
And he got her a drink and he sent her to bed.
And when Cindy-Lou *Who* went to bed with her cup,
HE went to the chimney and stuffed the tree up!

Then the *last* thing he took
Was the log for their fire!
Then he went up the chimney, himself, the old liar.
On their walls he left nothing but hooks and some wire.

And the one speck of food
That he left in the house
Was a crumb that was even too small for a mouse.

Then

He did the *same* thing
To the *other Whos'* houses

Leaving crumbs
Much too small
For the other *Whos'* mouses!

It was quarter past dawn...

  All the *Whos,* still a-bed,

  All the *Whos,* still a-snooze

When he packed up his sled,

Packed it up with their presents! The ribbons! The wrappings!

The tags! And the tinsel! The trimmings! The trappings!

Three thousand feet up! Up the side of Mt. Crumpit,
He rode with his load to the tiptop to dump it!
"Pooh-Pooh to the *Whos!*" he was grinch-ish-ly humming.
"They're finding out now that no Christmas is coming!
"They're just waking up! I know *just* what they'll do!
"Their mouths will hang open a minute or two
"Then the *Whos* down in *Who*-ville will all cry BOO-HOO!

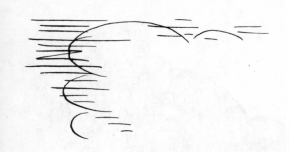

"That's a noise," grinned the Grinch,
"That I simply MUST hear!"
So he paused. And the Grinch put his hand to his ear.
And he did hear a sound rising over the snow.
It started in low. Then it started to grow...

inspire

But the sound wasn't *sad!*
Why, this sound sounded *merry!*
It *couldn't* be so!
But it WAS merry! VERY!

He stared down at *Who*-ville!
The Grinch popped his eyes!
Then he shook!
What he saw was a shocking surprise!

Every *Who* down in *Who*-ville, the tall and the small,
Was singing! Without any presents at all!

He HADN'T stopped Christmas from coming!
IT CAME!
Somehow or other, it came just the same!

And the Grinch, with his grinch-feet ice-cold in the snow,
Stood puzzling and puzzling: "How *could* it be so?
"It came without ribbons! It came without tags!
"It came without packages, boxes or bags!"
And he puzzled three hours, till his puzzler was sore.
Then the Grinch thought of something he hadn't before!
"Maybe Christmas," he thought, *"doesn't* come from a store.
"Maybe Christmas . . . perhaps . . . means a little bit more!"

And what happened *then* . . . ?
Well . . . in *Who*-ville they say
That the Grinch's small heart
Grew three sizes that day!
And the minute his heart didn't feel quite so tight,
He whizzed with his load through the bright morning light
And he brought back the toys! And the food for the feast!
And he . . .

...HE HIMSELF...!

The Grinch carved the roast beast!

Books by Dr. Seuss
available with audio cassettes
from Random House:

THE CAT IN THE HAT
THE CAT IN THE HAT COMES BACK
DR. SEUSS'S ABC
FOX IN SOCKS
GREEN EGGS AND HAM
HOP ON POP
HOW THE GRINCH STOLE CHRISTMAS!
I CAN READ WITH MY EYES SHUT!
OH SAY CAN YOU SAY?
OH, THE THINKS YOU CAN THINK!
ONE FISH TWO FISH RED FISH BLUE FISH